The First Snowman

Andrea Sheree' Kemmerlin

Illustrated by Mikaila Maidment

The First Snowman

Andrea Sheree' Kemmerlin

Published by 1st World Publishing
P.O. Box 2211, Fairfield, Iowa 52556
tel: 641-209-5000 • fax: 866-440-5234
web: www.1stworldpublishing.com

First Edition

LCCN: 2013937892
SoftCover ISBN: 978-1-4218-8665-7
eBook ISBN: 978-1-4218-8666-4

Cover and Interior Illustrations: Mikaila Maidment

Deep in the woods of Oklahoma, a baby bunny slowly emerges from his burrow. His blue eyes begin to widen as he stares at a world he has never seen. His small pink nose twitches as he smells the winter air. The curious bunny reaches his paw towards the fluffy snow. THUD…a large clump of snow falls from a nearby tree and covers the baby bunny. He quickly shakes the snow off and begins to shiver.

"This white stuff is so cold," he said.

He crept back into his burrow and couldn't wait to tell his mama about his new discovery.

"Mama there is fluffy white stuff everywhere and some of it fell on my head!" the bunny shouted. She twitches her nose as she wipes the snow off his fur.

"Mama the sweet grass is gone and some of the white stuff is even on the trees!" he shouted.
She gently wraps a quilt around him and sits him on her lap.

"Calm down sweetie…it's only snow…winter has come. I have waited for this day so that I could share a story with you. A story about a baby snowflake that never gave up on what she wanted-even when it seemed impossible. Your Nana told me this story when I was your age."

The baby bunny snuggled his body closer to her as she told a story of long ago.

Winter had come and the fluffy white clouds filled the sky. The frigid air swirled around the clouds. A baby snowflake peeked over the cloud and stared in amazement. Her cheeks were rosy and her crystallized body sparkled like a star.

"So all I have to do is float through the winter sky?" she asked another snowflake.

"Yes…your job will be to introduce winter, the snowflake stated. Without any hesitation the snowflake announced, "ok I will do it!" Her crystalized body sparkled as she floated in the winter sky. She began to hear children giggling as she got closer to the ground.

"They look like they are having so much fun," she thought to herself.

"Hey watch where you are going!" an older snowflake shouted, as she fell to the ground.

"Oh…sorry sir I didn't mean to disturb you," the baby snowflake stated.

She looked up and could see a multitude of baby snowflakes float through the sky.

"Do we just lay here until winter is over?" she asked the older snowflake. "Oh great…I happen to get stuck next to a talkative snowflake all winter," the older snowflake murmured.

More than anything she wanted to have fun with the children. "I must get over there somehow," she thought to herself.

"Excuse me sir, could you please help me get closer to the children?" she asked the older snowflake. He slowly opened his eyes and stated, " That would be impossible and you need to give up on your silly idea. Your job is to lie here all winter and to be quite so I can sleep."

She struggled to pull herself up but nothing seemed to work. "Even when things look bad, you must never give up," she thought to herself. With all her might she pulled herself up. Her face lit up as she balanced herself on one of her crystallized points. THUD…all of a sudden a brisk wind knocked her flat on her face.

"Oh no I have a problem," she stated in a muffled voice.

The older snowflake quickly opened his eyes and began to laugh. "I knew you wouldn't be able to do it," the older snow-flake stated. She knew that he was wrong and she wasn't about to give up

The baby snowflake struggled to pull herself up again and it worked! She balanced herself on one of her crystallized points and rolled herself forward.

"Hey what are you supposed to be?" a baby bunny asked. "I'm a baby snowflake," she stated.
The baby bunny began to laugh so hard that she fell on her back.

"What is so funny?" she asked the bunny. "You are a funny look-ing snowflake and you look more like a snowball." The bunny said.
She quickly looked down and noticed that she was a snowball.

"Could you please help me to get closer to the children?" she asked. 'I'm such a small bunny but I can try."

The baby bunny began to push the snowball with all her might. She pushed and pushed the snowball and soon felt like giving up.

The baby bunny sat down next to the snowball and let out a long sigh. She put one of her arms around the snowball and said,

"I want to give up because pushing you is too hard for me. I'm not big enough and it seems impossible."

"Nothing is impossible when you put your mind to it and I believe in you!" the snowball shouted with such excitement.

The baby bunny quickly stood up and said, "no one has ever believed in me. I always get into trouble at home and I hop slower than my brothers."

The two began their journey again and the bunny pushed the snowball with all her might.

"Hey what are you supposed to be?" a snowflake asked. "I'm a... well I use to be a baby snowflake and now I'm a big snowball. I'm going to the bottom of this valley where the children play," she replied.

"Oh...how fun, may I join you?" the baby snowflake asked.

Soon the baby bunny was pushing both snowballs towards the valley.

"Watch where you are going!" a snowflake yelled.

"I'm sorry little snowflake, I'm trying to help my snowball friends get to the bottom of this valley," the baby bunny said. The snowflake rose her eyes up and stared at the large snow ball staring back at her. She then looked over at the other snow ball and noticed that she was much smaller.

"Can I join you?" the snowflake asked.

Soon the baby bunny was pushing three snowballs closer to the children.

"Why did we stop?" the biggest snowball asked. "I can see a yummy carrot at the bottom of the valley," the baby bunny said as she twitched her pink nose.

"You can get the carrot later," the biggest snowball stated.

"I have worked so hard pushing snowballs and that carrot looks so tasty. Stay right here and I will be right back," the bunny said. Before the snowballs could say anything the bunny was jumping down the valley towards the carrot.

"We can do the rest on our own," the biggest snowball stated. "I don't know...I think we should just wait for the bunny to come back," the smaller snowball stated.

"All we have to do is roll down this hill and we will be where the children are," the biggest snowball explained.

Without hesitation the biggest snowball began to roll down the hill. Soon all three snowballs were rolling down the hill. They began to roll so fast that they were unable to see where they were going. The baby bunny quickly looked up and put the tasty carrot down. Her eyes got wider as the snowballs came closer. THUD…the snowballs fell onto the bunny. She began to struggle to get out from under the snowballs. With her hands placed on her hips—she twitched her pink nose in confusion.

The snowballs tried to lift themselves up with all their might. The baby bunny lifted her head in amazement and began to laugh so hard that she fell on her back.

"What is so funny?" the biggest snowball asked.

"You should see yourself…there are two walnuts for eyes, my carrot looks like a nose, and there are two branches on your side that look like arms!" the bunny shouted.

Just then the children stopped giggling, and ran towards the strange figure.

"What is that?" an older girl asked. "It's a snowman!" a little boy shouted.

Soon a multitude of baby snowflakes began to fall from the sky, as the children gathered closer to the snowman.

"No matter what…I never gave up," the snowman thought to herself.

The mama bunny held her baby bunny closer. "Mama, was the baby bunny in the story my Nana?" he asked.

"Yes it was sweetie. That is how the first snowman came to be, and ever since then children make snowmen when it snows," she said.

"Where is my sweet grandbaby?" a familiar voice asked. "Nana!" the baby bunny shouted as he hopped towards her. "Nana can we please go outside and make a snowman together?" the baby bunny asked. She held her grandson close and smiled.

"I would love to make a snowman with you," she said.

This book is dedicated to my wonderful children and grand-children. I also dedicate this book to every child who has ever attended McClure Elementary School in Tulsa, Oklahoma. I want to thank everyone who believed in me—I never gave up!